TIDGIE'S INNINGS

and other stories

Tidgie's Innings

AND OTHER STORIES

V H Drummond

HUTCHINSON
London   Sydney   Auckland   Johannesburg

Random Century Australia Pty Ltd 20 Alfred Street, Sydney, NSW
2016

Random Century New Zealand Ltd PO Box 40–086, Glenfield,
Auckland 10, New Zealand

Random Century South Africa (Pty) Ltd PO Box 337, Bergvlei,
2012, South Africa

Typeset by Deltatype Limited, Ellesmere Port
Printed and bound in Great Britain by Mackays of Chatham PLC,
Chatham, Kent

British Library Cataloguing in Publication Data
Drummond, V. H. (Violet Hilda), 1911–
Tidgie's innings and other stories.
I. Title
832.912 (J)
ISBN 0–09–174248–X

Contents

BOOK ONE

Tidgie's Innings

TIDGIE'S INNINGS

Miss Sprot was an assistant in the Toy Department of a big London store. One evening a large packing case arrived.

Out of it Miss Sprot took eleven cardboard boxes, with eleven velvet dogs in them. Each dog was dressed in a blue cap and a blue blazer with yellow piping.

'Why! It's a cricket team,' cried Miss Sprot. 'The Wouffle Ramblers!'

Next she unpacked eleven furry bears dressed in red and black caps and red and black blazers.

'Another cricket team!' cried Miss Sprot. 'The E-Zonga-Bee!'

Miss Sprot arranged them in two rows facing each other. Then she put on her hat and went home.

Now that the shop was empty, the captain of the dogs' team, Snootie Fanshawe, spoke. 'Fancy coming face to face with a rotten team like the E-Zonga-Bee in a Toy Department!'

He laughed scornfully.

The Wouffle Ramblers then started boasting

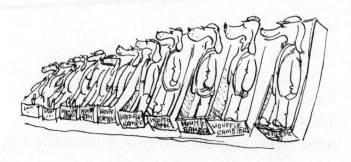

about how many matches they had won and what a wonderful team they were.

The bears were amazed, they were never conceited or boastful.

'The E-Zonga-Bee is a fine team,' said their captain, Philip Watson, quietly.

'Our captain is a fine fellow,' cried the bears.

'I'm a fine fellow too,' barked Snootie Fanshawe.

'Bet you could not beat us,' barked one of the dogs.

'Bet we could,' growled the bears.

'Let's have a match,' cried Philip Watson.

'Then we'll soon see who's the best team!'

So the E-Zonga-Bee challenged the Wouffle Ramblers, who eagerly accepted the challenge. They were all keen to play straight away, and tried to scramble from their cardboard boxes, but they were tied in and could not move.

But they were not to be put off. They decided that after they were sold they would creep out of their new homes and play the match in the Park on the night of the first full moon in June.

Some bath toys sat on a shelf near by, a Muscovy Duck and a Swan.

'I will come and fetch the E-Zonga-Bee,' said the Muscovy Duck. 'They can sit on my back and fly to the Park. My friend, the Swan, I'm sure, will collect the Wouffle Ramblers. We would love an adventure like this.'

The Swan did not look so very keen, but she graciously agreed to do it.

A China Pig in a china sailor suit took a little step

forward. 'I'll be the umpire,' he said.

'I'll keep the score,' said a Jointed Horse. 'With my jointed front hoof I can write quite nicely.'

The only person who did not seem at all interested in all this was a rather small bear called Tidgie Widgie. In spite of his smart blazer and cap, he hated cricket and was very bad at it. All he wanted was to be bought by a little girl who would love him, and take him around with her.

He did not like the idea of a moonlight cricket match at all.

In the morning they were awakened by Miss Sprot flicking about with a feathery mop.

The customers arrived and a little girl came in. Tidgie hoped that she would buy him, but, to his great disappointment, she chose

Crackers Nutsford, the wicket keeper.

Miss Sprot wrote the little girl's name and address in a book called ON ACCOUNT. The Muscovy Duck peered from her shelf and read the address.

'In this way,' she said to the Swan, 'we shall know where to fetch each one for the moonlight cricket match.'

Whenever a little girl came in Tidgie tried to look pleasant and charming, but somehow a bulbous balloon had slipped in front of him, hiding his face from view. So when closing time

came, each member of both teams had been sold, and only poor Tidgie remained.

In the morning Miss Sprot arranged some games of skill in the place where the cricket teams had been. She attached the bulbous balloon to a little lorry that was full of cricket bats and balls and stumps.

Now only Tidgie's toes could be seen.

'Never mind,' whispered the Muscovy Duck.

'You looked attractive as a team, but one bear in cricketing clothes is nothing special.'

Tidgie felt very forlorn.

Just then a little boy in a red coat came in. He took a great fancy to the bulbous balloon, so his uncle bought it for him. The little lorry with the cricket stumps got tangled up with the balloon cords so the uncle bought that too. Then he

bought the bath Swan and lastly the Muscovy
Duck. The little boy staggered away from the
department with all his purchases.

Tidgie suddenly felt happier. Now he could see
and be seen. And if he was sold there would be no
Muscovy Duck to find out where he lived to take
him to the moonlight cricket match!

A lady wearing a white flower came into the
Toy Department.

'I want a teddy bear, please,' she said.

Miss Sprot showed her many bears, both large
and small, but she did not seem to like any of them
much. Then her eye alighted on Tidgie.

'He will do fine,' she said. 'Don't bother to
wrap him up.'

She put him under her arm and hurried to the lift.

'Ground floor, street level!' said the lift attendant. 'Millinery! Hosiery! Confectionery! Haberdashery!'

They hurried through all the departments mentioned till they came to a revolving door.

Twice round the revolving door they revolved! When, at last, they got to the street the lady called 'Taxi! Taxi!' But no taxi stopped.

A doorman, standing by, put two fingers to his

mouth and made a loud shrill whistle which brought a taxi to the spot immediately.

'Please go to Number 18 Margaret Square,' said the lady to the taxi driver.

At this moment the little boy in the red coat emerged from the shop carrying his presents.

The Muscovy Duck craned inquisitively forward.

'She has heard where I'm going,' thought Tidgie anxiously. 'Now she'll know where to come for me for the moonlight cricket match!'

But he was too excited to worry for long.

The lady tapped on the driver's window with Tidgie's nose.

'Drive fast, please,' she said.

When they arrived at Number 18 Margaret Square they were greeted from the balcony by a pretty little girl and her mother.

'I'm afraid I'm late,' said the lady. 'I've bought you this cricketing bear, Sarah.'

The parlourmaid came up from the basement and opened the front door. Sarah came running down the stairs. She hugged Tidgie and seemed very pleased with him.

They all went up to the nursery for tea. Sarah showed Tidgie to Nannie.

'Isn't he sweet?' she said. During tea Tidgie sat on Sarah's right. On her other side sat a dilapidated-looking creature called Minky who had only one ear, one eye and one arm. He flopped forward on to the table because so much stuffing had come out of his body that he could neither sit nor stand.

The lady gave Sarah the flower she was wearing to put in Tidgie's button-hole. Sarah fed him with milk from her own cup and titbits of buttered scone and very small slices of chocolate cake. She carefully wiped his chin if crumbs got stuck in the fur there.

Tidgie thought of the rest of the team; none of them could be happier than he, sitting here in this cosy nursery, with a huge flower tickling his nose, being fed with dainty morsels by a little girl.

When the grown-ups had gone Sarah showed him round her nursery. They played with her trains, her dolls' house and her Noah's ark.

He thought that she was the sweetest little girl in the world and he was the luckiest bear.

When bedtime came Nannie told Sarah to tidy up her toys. To his great disgust Tidgie got tidied up with the rest and put in a cupboard. As Nannie was closing the cupboard door he was dismayed to see Sarah going off with the crumpled Minky in her arms.

A lovely doll in a sprigged muslin dress asked him his name.

'I'm Queenie,' she said.

She told him that they had all been there for months and months.

'It's very dull sitting here all day long,' she said. 'Minky is the only one who has any fun. Sarah takes him everywhere. He travels with her, he sits beside her at all meals and even goes to parties with her.'

The other toys nodded their heads wearily.

'She loves him dearly,' went on Queenie. 'Nannie washes his shirt once a week . . . our clothes are never washed because we never do anything to make them dirty. Your flannels will be as clean this time next year as they are today. Sometimes Minky himself is washed and hung in the airing cupboard. That is one of the reasons why his stuffing is so relaxed.'

Tidgie was worried. 'I think she quite likes me,' he said. 'We played together the whole evening. At tea she gave me a flower.'

'She played with us all when we first arrived, and then into the cupboard we go and are forgotten,' said Queenie.

At this, huge tears rolled out of Tidgie's eyes

and fell on to his blazer.

'Never mind,' said Queenie, lending him her handkerchief. 'We all cried at first, but you'll get over it.'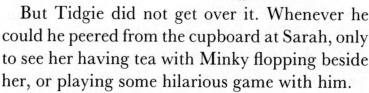

But Tidgie did not get over it. Whenever he could he peered from the cupboard at Sarah, only to see her having tea with Minky flopping beside her, or playing some hilarious game with him.

He watched her being got ready to go to the Park with Minky always clutched in one hand.

He asked the other
toys what Minky was
supposed to be. Some said
he had been a cat, some
thought a rabbit, but most
of them thought he had
been a donkey and the tuft
on his head was the remains of an ear.

One day as Nannie was tidying the cupboard,
Tidgie fell out on to the floor. He lay there hoping
Sarah would pick him up and pet him after his
fall.

Sarah came running into the nursery with
Minky in her hand. She stumbled over Tidgie and
fell on top of Minky.

Nannie picked them all up.

'Poor Tidgie,' said Sarah, and putting his cap on straight, replaced him in the cupboard.

Then she went to Nannie's rag-bag, and taking out all the prettiest pieces of rag carefully bandaged Minky up in them.

'Poor Minky,' she said. 'He's badly wounded.'

Tidgie sadly watched this proceeding. Queenie tried to comfort him, but he felt his heart was broken for ever.

That afternoon while Sarah was sitting in the Park a funny dog came bounding up to her, turning somersaults and showing off. She held Minky up to watch these amusing antics.

When the dog saw Minky he leapt at him and seized him.

Sarah screamed.

'Drop him! Drop him!' cried Nannie, pointing a stern finger at the dog, who took no notice but continued to pivot and prance with the unfortunate Minky dangling from his mouth.

Some people congregated to stare and Mr Green the Park Keeper came to see what was happening.

When he saw Mr Green, that mischievous dog raced away with the wretched Minky still in his mouth. Mr Green gave chase, followed by a small crowd with Nannie and Sarah bringing up the rear, through the Park and round the Tea Gardens.

Round the Tea Gardens they chased that
naughty dog.

The people in the Tea Gardens were interested in the chase but they were too busy eating buns and pastry to join in.

The chase ended by a lake called the Serpentine. The dog raced on the Serpentine Bridge and up on to the parapet, but as Mr Green approached

he let go of Minky, who rolled off the parapet into the water below. Sarah burst into tears. 'Minky has fallen into the Serpentine,' she cried.

The people echoed her words.

'Minky has fallen into the Serpentine!'
When he saw how distressed Sarah was, the dog decided to rescue Minky and, taking a deep breath through his long nose, dived into the water.

Minky glided downstream with his tuft floating on the surface of the water and his one eye gazing tragically to the heavens.

Another dog saw him and decided that he would like him as a plaything so he, too, dived into the water.

Both dogs reached Minky at the same time and proceeded to fight for him. They boxed each other and slapped and splashed, and the result was that Minky sank to the bottom of the Serpentine and was never seen again.

The two dogs swam to the shore, shook themselves all over the spectators and chased each other across the Park.

Nannie hurried Sarah home. When her mother heard the story she went to the cupboard and got out the other toys. 'Now, Sarah,' she said, 'which one will sit beside you at tea today?'

Tidgie hoped and hoped that she would choose him; but Sarah just cried and said she did not want any of them.

That night the toys were very excited, each one hoping that he would be chosen as Sarah's favourite. But Tidgie had given up all hope and pushing the cupboard door open with his toe, gazed mournfully out of the window.

Suddenly he saw the full moon appearing over the houses on the other side of the square.

He gasped, remembering with dismay the cricket match to be played on the night of the first full moon in June.

A dark shadow appeared against the moon . . .
the Muscovy Duck! She slowly circled round the
Square. As she drew nearer, Tidgie saw the

E-Zonga-Bees sitting on her back, waving their bats and shouting: 'Tidgie! Tidgie! Come out and play cricket!'

Tidgie tried to hide in the corner of the cupboard, but the Muscovy Duck tapped with her beak on the window till all the toys woke up.

'Does a bear called Tidgie Widgie live here?' asked Philip Watson.

'Why, yes,' cried Queenie.

The toys, thinking he was lucky to go for a moonlight flight with his friends, helped him on to the duck's back. The Muscovy Duck flapped her wings and away they went.

As they flew over the Great City the bears talked of the adventures they had had since they left the Toy Department. They had all had wonderful times with their children, going to the seaside and to parties, and playing in the Park.

Tidgie kept quiet.

He looked down at the darkened city and the twinkling lights below.

Suddenly Philip Watson shouted, 'There's the Park! And there are the Wouffle Ramblers flying towards us!'

The two teams greeted each other cordially in the sky, then they flew over the tree tops until they

had found a nice lawn to play on, not far from Mr
Green's lodge.

Down to the earth they dived; the cricketers
clung to their caps as the wind whistled past their
ears.

They sprang from the birds' backs and pushed
the stumps into the grass. The Muscovy Duck
had thoughtfully brought the stumps, bats and
balls from the toy lorry.

'No Umpire! Can't play,' said Tidgie, hopefully.

At once the cry was taken up.

'No Umpire! No Umpire!'

'No Scorer! Can't play!' said Tidgie.

Again the cry was taken up.

'No Scorer! No Umpire! No Umpire! No Scorer!'

Then a great clattering was heard, accompanied by the thud of small horses' hooves and, across the Park, from out of the west, the Jointed Horse came galloping with the China Pig on his back. Behind them they dragged a toy cart with a toy blackboard on it and a little sponge and a piece of chalk.

No one knew where they had come from or how they had got there, but everyone, except Tidgie, was delighted to see them.

The Jointed Horse set up his blackboard under a tree, and with his sponge in one hoof and his chalk in the other announced that he was ready to score.

'Let us toss,' said the China Pig, and threw a shining penny high into the air with his trotter.

'Heads,' cried Snootie Fanshawe.

'Heads!' cried Philip Watson.

'You can't have heads too!' said Snootie Fanshawe angrily. 'I said it first.'

'Hush,' whispered the China Pig. 'It is unpleasant to quarrel at cricket.'

Snootie Fanshawe did not want to be considered an unpleasant cricketer so he said rather reluctantly: 'I'll have tails then.'

'I don't really mind,' said Philip Watson, 'I'll have tails.'

'Very well then,' said the China Pig. 'We'll toss for who has heads and who has tails.'

'Where is the penny?' said Philip Watson, looking on the ground. 'I can't see it.'

'Nor can I,' said Snootie Fanshawe.

'Nor can I,' said the China Pig.

It was tossed high in the air. It must have come down again, so the China Pig organized a hunt for it, but no one could see the shining penny.

The Muscovy Duck flew overhead.

'It's on the China Pig's hat,' she cried, with a quackle of laughter.

'Heads for the E-Zonga-Bee! Tails for the

Wouffle Ramblers!' cried the China Pig.

Both teams ran to look at his hat.

'It's tails!' quacked the Muscovy Duck.

So the Wouffle Ramblers went in first. Snootie Fanshawe was first to bat. He strolled proudly to the wicket, where Crackers Nutsford, the wicket keeper, awaited him.

Philip Watson bowled to him. He advanced so gracefully, so speedily and so brilliantly that he looked like a Catherine Wheel spinning round; but in spite of all his brilliance Snootie Fanshawe hit the ball and knocked it over the trees for six.

Philip Watson then bowled one of his famous

Lollipops . . . a very high ball, which lollied in the air and then landed pop on the wicket. Alas, this time it lollied in the air all right but did not pop on to Fanshawe's wicket; instead he took a mighty swipe at it and knocked it over the trees again.

Philip Watson continued to bowl fast or trickily, but without success, for Snootie Fanshawe hit every ball for six every time.

When it was Hamish Gordon's
turn to bowl he took off his
blazer and cap and handed them
to the China Pig. Most of the
bears followed suit. The China
Pig put the caps on his head
and the blazers round his neck.

Hamish bowled slowly, but
with great skill, to a dog called
Runge.

Runge hit the ball, but only far enough to run
one run, so Snootie Fanshawe faced the bowling
again. He took the slow balls and hit them almost
as far as the eye could see. He hardly ever
bothered to run because he always hit boundaries.

Philip Watson made every bear bowl in turn
but no one could get Snootie Fanshawe out. At
the end of an hour he and Runge had made two
hundred and twenty two runs between them.

The E-Zonga-Bee were very anxious.

Tidgie had been told to play longstop. He was far from the wicket, and, as no ball had come his way, he got a bit bored.

At his feet some daisies grew. Tidgie picked them. 'I'll make a little daisy chain for Sarah,' he said to himself.

He became so absorbed in this work that he forgot all about the cricket match till he heard a stern voice shout: 'Widgie! Get UP!'

He turned to see Philip Watson standing over him, his paws clenched and his eyes blazing with displeasure.

'Widgie,' he said. 'Remember that you are a cricketer and, above all, a member of the E-Zonga-Bee!'

Tidgie got up and hung his head. The dogs opened their huge mouths and laughed and laughed. The bears stared with scorn and rage to think that he had let their team down in this way.

'You had better come and bowl, it's your turn,' said Philip Watson offhandedly.

Tidgie walked to the wicket, his head bowed and a daisy still hanging from his lip.

'I'll show them,' he said to himself. 'I'll be the one to bowl Snootie Fanshawe out!'

He then advanced down the pitch, spinning and twisting and turning in the manner in which he had seen Philip Watson performing.

'I'm doing very well,' he said to himself.

Faster and faster he went, turning somersaults, bounding round and round . . . on and on. He really had not got the slightest idea where he was going . . . till he felt a horrible bump, and, looking

up, found himself gazing into the mocking face of Snootie Fanshawe. He had bounded about so vigorously and capered around so wildly that he had got all the way down the pitch without bowling the ball! Surprised and dismayed, he fell to the ground.

As he lay there, he heard the scornful laughter of the Wouffle Ramblers. Crackers Nutsford put his paws to his face with shame to think that a member of the E-Zonga-Bee could make such a fool of himself. Tidgie felt red under his face fur. The voice of his captain rang out across the pitch: 'Widgie! Get UP!'

He got up, feeling foolish, and walked slowly to the other wicket.

This time he bowled carefully and deliberately without any preliminary bounding or skipping.

But Snootie Fanshawe gave the ball a mighty
swipe straight back at him, sending him whizzing
into the air.

Again he fell backwards
to the ground and again
he heard the voice
of his captain shout:
'Widgie! Get UP!'

'Throw the
ball, Tidgie
Widgie,'
yelled the bears.
'Fanshawe is running
a run!'

Tidgie sat up, feeling dazed. But Munchy
Smith, a smart fielder, ran speedily to him, seized
the ball and hurled it very energetically to
Crackers Nutsford.

Meanwhile, Snootie Fanshawe was running
haughtily up and down the wicket. When he saw

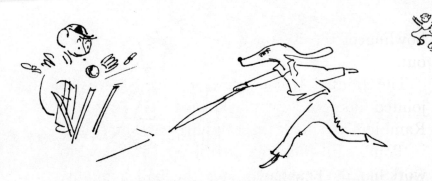

the quick work of Munchy he put on a terrific spurt . . . but Crackers Nutsford was too quick for him and swept the bails off the stumps just before he got back to the crease.

'How's that?' cried Crackers.

'How's that?' echoed the Bears.

'OUT,' said the China Pig.

The Muscovy Duck and the Swan, who had perched themselves on a tree to watch the match, clapped their wings and cried: 'Well fielded!'

As Tidgie was getting up from the grass, Philip Watson strode over to him and said, 'Widgie, you have let the side down.'

Then he turned and said, 'Well played, Nutsford and Smith!'

Crackers Nutsford and Munchy Smith stood about looking self-conscious and happy.

The rest of the Wouffle Ramblers then went in one by one, but the quick fielding and the fast bowling of the E-Zonga-Bee soon got them all out.

The Jointed Horse wrote the score with his jointed hoof on the blackboard. The Wouffle Ramblers had made three hundred and fifty runs.

'Pouf!' said Philip Watson. 'We shall have to work hard to beat that!'

Just then the Muscovy Duck flew down from the tree.

'You must go home now,' she said. 'For the

moon has gone and the sun is rising. If Mr Green finds us in the Park there will be trouble!'

But the cricketers refused to go until they had finished the match.

'Can't you see how dangerous it is?' hissed the Swan. 'The keepers might throw us into the rubbish cart, or strange children might run away with us!'

'If you are so foolish,' quacked the Muscovy Duck, 'we will go home without you.'

Then the captains lined up their teams and said: 'Paws up those who dare to stay in the Park and finish the match!'

All paws shot up except Tidgie's, who whispered, 'I would rather go home with the Muscovy Duck.'

'Twenty-one to one,' said Philip Watson,

looking scornfully at Tidgie.

'You will never find your way without us,' said
the Muscovy Duck. 'We'd better stay and take
you home but we don't like it!'

They went back to the tree murmuring,
'Foolish Bears! Foolish Dogs! We don't like it! We
don't like it!'

Then the E-Zonga-Bee went in. They batted
with great vigour and skill, and Philip Watson
made even more runs than Snootie Fanshawe.
The sun rose higher and higher. Then, yawning
and stretching in the morning air, Mr Green
appeared out of his lodge to open the Park Gates.

The sight of Mr Green was too much for the
Muscovy Duck. She came screeching from the
tree, followed by the Swan, who was twittering
with nervous fright.

'Come away! Come away!' they squawked. But
the cricketers took no notice. So the birds flew off
leaving them to their fate in the Park.

Imagine Mr Green's surprise when he saw some little toys earnestly playing cricket on the grass. But Mr Green had seen so many strange things in the Park that he was not as surprised as he might have been. He was very keen on cricket, so instead of bundling them away, he drew up a chair to watch the match and invited some ticket collectors to join him. He clapped his hands and shouted, 'Well played! Good shot!'

Then came the people and the children who walk in the Park. They all stared with amazement at the cricket match.

'Look,' they cried, clustering round. 'Some teddy bears and some toy dogs playing cricket!

This is indeed a strange sight to see!'

At last all the bears had batted and there was only Tidgie left to go in.

'Twenty-four runs to make to win the match,' cried Philip Watson.

'You'll never do it with Widgie at the wicket,' sneered Snootie.

The E-Zonga-Bee were in despair; they were sure Tidgie would be bowled first ball and they would lose the match.

Tidgie walked to the wicket with his bat in his paw. He hated cricket and he hated this moment more than any other. He shivered and shook with fright and his poor little furry knees trembled.

He glanced nervously at the crowd. Suddenly to his great joy he saw Sarah and Nannie standing in the front row. Sarah smiled at him in a very encouraging way. At once Tidgie's fright left him and his furry knees ceased to tremble.

Now he knew that Sarah was watching him, he felt as brave as a lion and was determined to make twenty-four runs.

Snootie Fanshawe bowled to him. He hit the ball with a mighty swipe in a backwards swerve that went over the Park Gates and hit a policeman on the helmet in the Bayswater Road.

The policeman graciously fielded the ball and the crowd clapped loudly.

Next Tidgie made a fine shot which landed in the chimney of Mr Green's lodge. Mr Green kindly climbed on to the roof after it. 'Well fielded,' cried the crowd.

Between each of these magnificent shots

Tidgie bowed to Sarah
and grinned at her.
Sarah smiled back
and clapped her
hands.

The next ball
went into the flower bed and the
Wouffle fielder had to climb the
railings and crawl carefully
amongst the flowers to find it.

Tidgie's last and most amazing shot went over
the trees and was heard to splash into the
Serpentine. One of the fielders had to take off his
shirt and dive in after the ball, which he could not
find in spite of splashing and growling about in

the water for some time. But nobody cared, for Tidgie had hit four boundaries for six.

The E-Zonga-Bee had won the match!

The rest of the team rushed to Tidgie and patted him on the back, and shook him by the paw. 'Well played, Tidgie Widgie!' cried Philip Watson.

Tidgie felt very proud.

Then the children ran forward to collect their toys. They were all too pleased to have them back to scold them for running away.

Sarah picked up Tidgie. 'I am very proud of you,' she said, and kissed him.

As she carried him off all the crowd cheered him.

For ever after, Sarah took Tidgie with her wherever she went, right until she was quite a grown-up girl.

He went with her to the Park, he travelled to the seaside and country with her, he even went to parties with her, and he always sat next to her at meals.

Nannie often had to wash him and hang him up in the airing cupboard.

He was always happy and he never, never played cricket again.

Lady
Talavera

LADY TALAVERA

In a field in Talavera Park lived an old sheep called Caroline.

One winter's day she decided to take her two new lambs, Sousa and Elly, for their first walk. 'I want to test your legs,' she said. 'To make sure that they are not so wonky as they look.'

The two lambs tottered and stumbled but managed quite well with a few pushes and nudges from Caroline.

'We will go as far as that myrtle bush,' she said.

When they got to the myrtle bush they were surprised to find another lamb lying there in a faint and exhausted condition.

'I am an orphan,' wept the lamb. 'I fear I shall die of exposure.'

'You will not!' cried Caroline. 'For I will look after you and bring you up with Sousa and Elly.'

Caroline called her Myrtle, because it was under a myrtle bush that she found her.

They made their home under the myrtle bush. Caroline liked its position because from there she could see Talavera House where Lady Talavera lived.

Caroline's family had always lived on this estate; they had served the Talaveras with good wool for generations. Caroline was very proud of this fact, and it pleased her to be in constant view of the stately house. She particularly liked to watch Lady Talavera driving in her car, and wonder if she was wearing any garment made from her own fine wool.

Myrtle soon recovered from her exposure, and all the lambs' legs grew strong and woolly, so that when spring came they were able to run and skip in all directions.

But Myrtle was not always happy, in spite of the great kindness of Caroline, for as she grew older it became very noticeable that she was much smaller than the other sheep and lambs in the flock.

Because of this, the other lambs jeered and mocked her.

Myrtle hated this treatment and became more and more self-conscious; she could hardly bear to appear amongst the flock.

'Go, Myrtle . . . join the frolicking and frisking,' said Caroline, but she could not, for fear of

the jeering and mocking that would greet her.

She found a little stream where she could see her reflection. 'I am different from the others,' she sighed, and wept into the water.

At last, because she could bear it no longer, she decided to run away.

'I won't run too far,' she said to herself. 'I shall get back to Caroline by nightfall.'

She escaped while they were resting under the myrtle bush. None of the others noticed her.

She ran through the park, across fields and over small hills.

She came to a little house at the bottom of a little wood.

With great daring she ran down the path till she came to the front door.

A man was sitting there, leaning against a green water butt.

'What a nice expression your house has,' said Myrtle.

'It is the keeper's lodge and I am the keeper,' replied the man.

'What do you keep?' asked Myrtle.

'I keep care of that gate,' answered the man, whose name was Mr Charabin.

63

'What do you have to do?'

'I have to open it for Lady Talavera when she wishes to drive through.'

'Does she come through often?' asked Myrtle.

'Not often. She only came through twice last year. I am not a very busy man,' replied Mr Charabin. 'There are six gates to Talavera Park, and this is the smallest and most unimportant, and this lodge is the smallest and most insignificant.'

He told her about the magnificent Main Gate, which was made of wrought iron, and had two fabulous creatures sitting on either side. 'I had dearly hoped to be keeper of that gate one day, but alas, just before the other keeper retired, they made the Main Gate automatic. It works by an Invisible Bump in the road; as soon as Lady Talavera's car passes over this bump, the magnificent gates swing open, and when it passes over the Invisible Bump on the other side, they automatically swing to again,' he said. 'After the Main Gates became automatic, they did not have a keeper any more; and now that elegant lodge stands empty.'

He went on to describe the elegant lodge which had bay windows and a porch with ornamental columns.

'Ah! How my wife and I had longed to live in that lodge,' he sighed. 'I have seldom smiled or laughed since that gate became automatic.'

Just then the little lodge started to shake and tremble.

'Why does it do that?' asked Myrtle as they leapt away.

When it had stopped Mr Charabin said:

'Alas, it is my son, Nicholas. Every time Nicholas sneezes the house shakes.'

'But why does Nicholas sneeze so often?' said Myrtle.

'It is his dreadful colds,' sighed Mr Charabin.

'If he had a nice coat like mine he would not catch colds,' said Myrtle, pivoting round and round to show off her wool.

'True,' answered Mr Charabin, 'but last winter Nick fell through the ice while sliding on a pond, and lost his coat. He has had a cold ever since, for I am too poor to buy him another.'

When Myrtle heard this she was dismayed. 'He can have my coat,' she cried. 'I run and skip too fast to catch colds.'

At this Mr Charabin was overjoyed. 'Thank you, you sweet creature!' he cried, and ran to fetch his shears.

He sheared off all the wool from Myrtle's body.

66

Then Mrs Charabin
appeared with her spin-
ning wheel and wove
a beautiful coat
with a little collar
from Myrtle's
tail wool,
leggings
from her leg
wool, and a little cap from her face wool.

'Oh thank you, dear lamb,' she cried as she
wove.

Myrtle felt naked and thin.

They carried the garments up to Nicholas's
room, where he was sneezing and making the
house shake again.

When he saw the beautiful coat and woolly
accessories he was overjoyed, and jumped from
his bed to have them tried on.

'Thank you, my dear lamb!' he cried.
They fitted him beautifully.
'Come on,' he said, 'let's play in the park.'
They played all sorts of games including swing-
ing on branches, and turning somersaults.

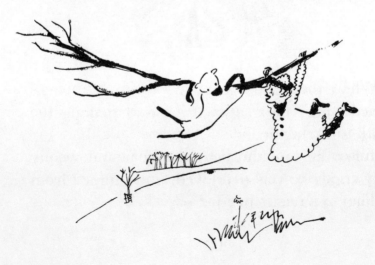

Then they sat down under a tree and Myrtle told him about the flock and how they had jeered and mocked at her because she was so small. Nicholas said that he thought her perfect. 'I wish you would stay with me for ever and ever,' he said. 'We could have such fun together.' Myrtle said that she would love it too, but she could not leave Caroline or Sousa and Elly.

When they got back a dreadful thing happened. . . . Myrtle sneezed. Luckily she was too weak to shake the lodge. 'She has caught a truly awful cold from going out without her coat on!' they cried, in great dismay.

They put her to bed for a week, and when she

was better they brought her down to the kitchen and sat her in front of the fire, wrapped in a pink bedjacket trimmed with swansdown.

Mrs Charabin made her some semolina to make her wool grow.

Mr Charabin lent her his own hot water bottle with **HOT WAT BOT** embroidered on the cover.

Nicholas put on his Myrtle wool coat and went out into the

spinney and gathered some primroses for her. But Myrtle was sad.

70

'Oh, dear! Oh, dear!' she sighed. 'Caroline will be so worried. I must get back to her.'

'You cannot go until you have grown a new coat,' they cried. 'You will catch another cold! It would be madness!'

Just then they heard a slight commotion outside. They popped their heads out of the window, and saw Lady Talavera alighting from her car with a large dress box under her arm.

71

'It looks as if she is coming in here,' they cried excitedly.

They quickly popped back into the kitchen. Nicholas smoothed down his hair, Mrs Charabin smoothed out her apron, while Mr Charabin combed his moustache with a good strong comb.

Then they rushed and opened the door, and Lady Talavera entered.

After they had chatted for some time, Lady Talavera opened the dress box; tissue paper fluttered all over the place.

'What could be inside?' they wondered.

Lady Talavera drew out a red, tailor-made coat, with a hat and leggings to match.

'It is for Nicholas,' she said, holding them up for all to see. 'Because I heard that he was sneezing and making the house shake.'

Everyone was delighted.

'Try it on! Try it on,' they cried eagerly. They did not like to mention that he already had a new coat, in case they offended her.

Unfortunately it was much too small. Everyone was bitterly disappointed, even Lady Talavera looked a bit crestfallen.

'What shall we do?' they asked, and no one could think of an answer.

Then Lady Talavera noticed Myrtle sitting demurely by the fire. 'Who is this?' she asked.

'It is Myrtle the lamb,' said Nick.

'Dressed in a pink bedjacket trimmed with swansdown?

How strange!' said Lady Talavera.

She was obviously very interested in Myrtle and asked so many questions that Nick told her the tale of the heroic way in which the little lamb had sacrificed her wool, so that he might play in the open air and get rid of his sneezes.

Lady Talavera was deeply moved by Myrtle's unselfish behaviour.

'I have a wonderful plan!' she cried. 'If Nicholas has the lamb's coat, why should not the lamb have Nicholas's coat?'

Everyone clapped their hands and agreed that this indeed was a brilliant plan.

'Try it on! Try it on,' they all cried eagerly.

They all decided that she looked charming in the tailor-made outfit and that she should keep it, it fitted her so well. She was enchanted with the gift.

'Now I can return to Caroline,' she said, 'for this beautiful outfit will keep me warm.'

Nicholas was sad. 'You'll never find your way,' he said. 'You'll get lost.'

Then Lady Talavera said that she would take her in the car and help her find the way, but seeing Nicholas's sad face she added: 'Would you like to come too, to find out where Myrtle lives so that you can go and visit her?'

Nicholas thought this was a lovely idea, and both he and Myrtle got quite excited.

Myrtle said good-bye to Mr and Mrs Charabin and thanked them for being so kind to her, and they thanked her for being so kind to them. Then Lady Talavera asked if it would be all right for her to take Nicholas with her, and they said 'Of course, of course,' and dressed him up in the Myrtle wool coat and cap and leggings.

'How smart he looks,' remarked Lady Talavera. 'I will bring him back shortly.'

'Look!' she said to Trundle, the chauffeur. 'Isn't this little lamb pretty? See how quaint she looks in her tailor-made outfit.'

Trundle looked coldly down: 'The little creature is very droll,' he remarked.

Lady Talavera then shuffled herself about in the car, pulling the rugs and foot-muffs round everyone; she decided that Myrtle should sit right inside one of the foot-muffs so that she should not be in a draught.

'Drive to the flock in the field in the park,' she said to Trundle.

There were a good many fields and flocks in Talavera Park and Trundle did not know which one to go to.

He stopped hopefully at one field. Myrtle peered out of her foot-muff. She could not recognize any of the faces of any of the sheep or lambs in the flock.

'Wrong field! Wrong flock!' she said.

Lady Talavera turned a little handle that let down the window in front.

'Wrong field! Wrong flock!' she said to Trundle.

Trundle said: 'Very good, my lady,' but put on a supercilious expression; he thought it was silly driving about with boys dressed as lambs and lambs dressed as boys.

They drove on to another field. Myrtle scanned the sheep's and lambs' faces for Caroline, Sousa or Elly, but could see no sheep or lamb she knew. 'Wrong field! Wrong flock!' she said.

'Wrong field! Wrong flock!' repeated Lady Talavera to Trundle. (This time she did not turn the handle, but spoke through the speaking trumpet.) The back of Trundle's head looked cross and disapproving of the whole business.

Myrtle grew anxious.

At last, craning her neck out of the foot-muff, she saw the myrtle bush not far off. Lady Talavera pointed it out to Trundle, who made the car race at eighty-two miles per hour.

'I wish he would always drive as fast as this!' said Lady Talavera.

When Caroline noticed Lady Talavera's car, she ran to have a look.

Stop! Stop!' cried Lady Talavera, rapping on the glass with her umbrella. Myrtle was so excited that she stood up in her muff.

Caroline had never seen Lady Talavera close to before, so when the car stopped she daringly poked her great woolly head inside. Imagine her surprise when she saw Myrtle sitting there

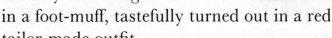

in a foot-muff, tastefully turned out in a red tailor-made outfit.

They greeted each other joyfully, while Trundle looked on, disdainfully holding the foot-muff.

'Well! You do look posh,' said Caroline. And Sousa and Elly eyed her with envious eyes.

Myrtle told them of her adventures and explained why she had not come back before.

Then Lady Talavera addressed the flock. She told them of Myrtle's noble act in sacrificing her coat so that Nick might run and play in the spring air. The flock were extremely impressed and Caroline felt very proud.

'She has got a new coat,' said Lady Talavera, 'but now that she is coming back to you, you must not jeer at her or mock her just because she is small.'

The flock bleated loudly to say that they were proud to have Myrtle with them; they had never had such a noble and smartly dressed lamb in their midst before.

Myrtle was happy to think that they would not jeer at her or mock her again.

Then Lady Talavera said to Nicholas: 'You must say goodbye to Myrtle, and for a treat I will take you to see the automatic gate.'

Nicholas was delighted, but he was loath to say goodbye to Myrtle.

'Perhaps Myrtle could come and see the gates, too,' said Lady Talavera, 'if Caroline could spare her a little.'

'Why, of course, my lady,' said Caroline, and all the time she was wondering if Lady Talavera was wearing any garment made from her own fine wool.

Lady Talavera touched her on the head and said, 'Your wool is so fine and soft that I think my hat, with this jade green plume, must be made from it. Never have I had a hat of such fine texture!' Caroline felt that this was the proudest and happiest day in her life.

She escorted them back, with Myrtle, to the car, and curtsied, in her own special sheepish way, as they departed.

They drove to the automatic gate, and sure enough it was just as Mr Charabin had described, with the two fabulous creatures sitting on either side; and there was the elegant lodge.

The exciting moment came when they went over the Invisible Bump. The magnificent gates swung majestically open, and into Talavera Park they sailed. Then, as they went over the Invisible Bump on the other side, the gates swung slowly to again. Nick and Myrtle were very impressed. 'Do

they work the same coming from the other way?'
they asked, breathlessly.

'Why, certainly they do!' replied Lady
Talavera, reaching for the speaking trumpet.
'Turn round, Trundle, and we will show them!'

Trundle turned the car. As he looked over his
shoulder they could see that he had a very sour
expression on his face. 'I shall be late for my tea,'
he said to himself. 'I am sick of dithering about
like this. . . . I shall drive as fast as I can, so as to
be back by tea-time.'

Faster and faster and faster he went, towards the gates . . . faster and faster! By the time they had got to the Invisible Bump the speed was terrific; but the gates, not being used to such furious driving, broke down under the strain. There was an ear-splitting crack, the automatic spring broke, and the gates flew open, completely out of control, in *opposite* directions! To and fro they clanged, making a tremendous noise as they did so.

Lady Talavera and party were in great peril. It

was only by sheer luck that they managed to whiz through without being squashed as the great gates swung apart.

Myrtle was tossed from the foot-muff to the floor. Some villagers, who heard the noise, came running to the spot.

'The magnificent gates of Talavera Park are broken!' they cried, in dismay.

Mr Charabin, hearing the commotion, put on his check cap and took Mrs Charabin to see what was happening.

They arrived to find that a workman with red braces had been sent for. He had dug up the Invisible Bump, and said that he could not mend the gate unless it could be made to close.

Trundle stood in the background looking crestfallen and foolish.

Lady Talavera said, 'My magnificent gates have turned into a public danger. If they don't stop clanging and swinging they may knock someone over, or, worse still, they may fly off their hinges and knock a small crowd down. Furthermore, I cannot possibly drive through them. What can be done?'

Nobody could answer. The situation was very grave. Everybody wished that they were brave enough to go near the gates for Lady Talavera's sake; but no one dared for fear of being squeezed and squashed.

Only one man was truly brave . . . it was Mr Charabin. With a beating heart he rushed forward and clutched the gates as they swung near together. All the villagers gasped. 'Come back!' they cried. 'You'll be knocked down or squeezed and squashed!'

With one mighty wrench he pulled them close together, and shut them fast. The force of the impact carried him off his feet. He was nervous lest his thumbs would get pinched, but in getting them out in time he fell with a dreadful bump on his poor head.

Sadly, they carried him away.

They took him into the lodge, and laid him upon an elegant sofa. When he opened his eyes and found himself lying there in the lodge of his dreams, he recovered immediately.

Lady Talavera said to him, 'I want to thank you for your courageous behaviour today. You have saved the lives of the crowd from danger, and also you have made it possible for me to return to Talavera House. I am annoyed with the automatic gate, it has imperilled everyone's lives today, so I shall tell the workman with the red braces to fill in the Invisible Bump, and take away the automaticness. I shall, from now on, have the gate opened in the old-fashioned way, which is

really much more dignified, and I should very much like it if you would be the one to open it, for ever after.'

At this Mr Charabin sat up on the elegant sofa and smiled and laughed for the first time since the gate became automatic. 'I am the happiest man in Talavera Park!' he shouted.

That very day the workman with the red braces took off the automaticness, and the gates opened and shut easily and gracefully as they had done in days gone by; and the Charabins moved into the elegant lodge. As it was such a big lodge they asked Caroline, Myrtle, Sousa and Elly to live with them. The three lambs often took Nicholas down to the field with the myrtle bush, to play with their old friends; but Caroline preferred to sit in the spacious garden of the lodge watching for Lady Talavera's car, and hoping that she would be wearing her red hat with the jade green plume.

And from then on, Trundle was never cross or supercilious, because he knew that it was his fault that the gates of Talavera Park got broken. Instead, he drives Lady Talavera just as fast as she likes over the countryside.

And now Mr Charabin smiles every time he opens the magnificent gates for Lady Talavera, which is sometimes as much as twice a day. He is happy because he is so busy, and because he lives in the elegant lodge. And the villagers say that the old-fashioned way of opening gates is really much nicer than these new-fangled automatic ideas.

BOOK THREE
Mrs Easter and the Storks

MRS EASTER
AND THE STORKS

Mrs Easter and her nephew, Billie Guftie, once went abroad. They stayed in a charming country called Denmark, with Mrs Easter's friends, Mr and Mrs Jensen.

Many of the houses in Denmark have storks' nests on their chimneys. Two big storks lived on Mr and Mrs Jensen's roof, a devoted married couple called Sally and Sam. Sally was a rare bird, she had a luminous beak, which shone most brightly at night.

Billie Guftie enjoyed his holiday, though he looked forward to the journey home in the S.S. *Queenie*, the great liner that lay in the harbour.

But on the day of their departure, a terrible tragedy was discovered; Sally, the Stork's wife, had disappeared during the night!

They all went up to the roof to try to comfort Sam.

'Sally has gone; seized or stolen!' they said mournfully, clustering round him in the nest.

'We will organize a search party for her,' said Mr Jensen. 'But first we must take Mrs Easter

and Billie Guftie to the harbour or they will miss the boat.'

So they descended from the roof and made their way towards the harbour, followed by the grieving bird.

When all goodbyes had been said, Mrs Easter and Billie Guftie walked up the gangway on to the S.S. *Queenie*. Mr Jensen helped them with the luggage. Then he ran back down the gangway to Mrs Jensen and Sam, to wave to the departing guests.

Mrs Easter and Billie Guftie stood on the deck

and waved back. But the S.S. *Queenie* did not move. After a while Billie Guftie got tired of waving and went off to explore the great liner.

On the Promenade Deck he saw a man promenading along with a large bird in his arms. As they approached him he was amazed to see that the bird was none other than the missing stork, Sally!

Billie Guftie spoke severely. 'Drop that bird, Sir! Drop her I say! Let her go free!'

The man smiled at him.

'She is quite happy,' he said. 'For I am Burton. You must have heard of Burton, the Chief Superintendent of the Great City Zoo! This bird is fortunate for I am taking her there. Down below I have my Star Spotted Van in which I captured her last night. When we arrive I shall put her into it again and we shall drive to the wonderful Zoo!'

So saying, he strolled leisurely on.

Sally certainly did not look unhappy but there was a wistful expression in her eye.

Billie Guftie fully realized that he could not rescue her single handed. Even Mrs Easter with her parasol would be powerless against such a man as Burton. So he ran to the side of the boat and called to his friends on the quay.

'Sally is here!' he shouted. 'Sally is on board.'

But they could not hear him.

Suddenly, without thinking what he was doing, he jumped on to the gangway and rushed down it towards them.

Mrs Easter gasped. 'Come back! Come back!' she cried. 'For the boat is about to sail!'

But Billie Guftie did not hear her, and as he reached the quay, the gangway rose in the air . . .

and with a loud hoot the S.S. *Queenie* turned and made for the open sea!

'What have I done?' he wailed.

Mr and Mrs Jensen came running up. 'Why did you leave the S.S. *Queenie*?' they asked.

Billie Guftie burst into tears and, flinging his arms round Sam's neck, told what had happened.

When Sam heard that his beloved wife was on board the S.S. *Queenie*, he lifted up his lovely wings and flew towards her.

Mrs Jensen screamed.

'Come back! Come back!' cried Mr Jensen. 'For Billie Guftie is still clinging to your neck!'

When Sam heard these words, he made as if to return to shore.

'No! No!' cried Billie Guftie, bravely, 'Take me with you to the S.S. *Queenie*!'

So the good
bird flew on.

Billie Guftie's position was perilous. He was
afraid of the dark swirling sea below him, but
somehow he managed to clamber on to Sam's
back, via his neck.

Meanwhile Mrs Easter was pacing the decks of
the S.S. *Queenie* in a state of great agitation. She
had already asked the captain to go back for Billie
Guftie; but he had refused politely, saying that
the *Queenie* was a proud ship who never went back
once she had started.

When Mrs Easter saw the great bird
approaching, she said to herself: 'That looks like

Sam. What can he be up to? And what on earth is that on his back?'

Imagine her surprise when the bird drew nearer and she saw that it was Billie Guftie sitting there!

She called out to Sam to alight upon the deck; but the S.S. *Queenie*, now that she had reached the open sea, was travelling faster and faster.

Sam tried valiantly to catch up, but the speed of the great liner was too much for him.

'Come on! Come ON!' Mrs Easter yelled frantically, waving her parasol to encourage him.

But alas! A strong wind came out of the sea and caught in her parasol. The next moment she was blown right off the deck!

The Captain and the passengers did not notice Mrs Easter's departure; they were all busy below.

Only Billie Guftie watched her, with fear in his heart, as the wind blew her first this way and then that way.

Sam took no notice of her, he thought she was doing it on purpose. It did not occur to him that

ladies could not fly.

Suddenly a terrific wind came roaring out of the sky. Billie Guftie thought it would surely blow Mrs Easter away for ever; but, by great good fortune, it blew her toward them. When she was just above them, she very cleverly closed her parasol and floated down, down, down.

'Well! Well! Here I am!' she said brightly, as she landed, with a little thud, on the stork's back.

With Mrs Easter beside him, Billie Guftie no longer felt afraid. As they travelled along he told her how he came to be on the stork's back.

Though the S.S. *Queenie* was far away over the ocean they managed to keep her always in sight.

The journey seemed very long. Billie Guftie was glad when Mrs Easter pointed her parasol and cried: 'Land Ahoy! Land Ahoy!'

Now it was nearly dark, but they could see the

skyline of the Great City and the bright lights of the S.S. *Queenie*.

As the liner entered the mouth of the river, an amazing thing happened; a beautiful light rose from her deck and twinkled like a star above her.

The S.S. *Queenie* disappeared up the river but the twinkling light rose high in the night sky.

'It must be Sally!' cried Billie Guftie. 'She has made a bold escape!'

They were surprised that instead of coming towards them, she seemed to be moving further away . . . over the Great City.

'Poor bird!' cried Mrs Easter. 'It is too dark for her to see us! She is lost!'

With a tremendous flapping of wings, Sam made a great spurt forward.

Sally was not very good at flying; unlike most storks she preferred strolling about or sitting down. Sam was afraid that her wings would get tired and that she would be forced to land. He dreaded what might happen to her in the crowds and in the traffic below.

'There she goes!' cried Mrs Easter, pointing her parasol.

In spite of the seriousness of the situation, Billie Guftie could not help feeling excited. What a wonderful experience to be speeding over the Great City on a stork's back, with Mrs Easter beside him!

Somehow they could not quite catch up with Sally, who darted and swerved nervously about. On and on they went, round chimney-pots and church spires, over the domes of civic buildings and the turrets of stately hotels.

Suddenly Billie Guftie cried, 'Look! LOOK! She's flying over the Royal Palace!'

But at that moment the little light started sinking lower and lower in the sky.

'She's fainted!' gasped Mrs Easter. 'She'll crash-land on the Palace roof! How awful!'

Sam flew as fast as his wings would carry him.

Somehow, by the greatest good fortune, Sally

just missed the roof, with its chimneys and turrets, and floated down in front of the Royal Palace.

It so happened that at this moment the King himself was taking an evening stroll. You can imagine how astonished he was to see a fainting stork, with a luminous beak, fall at his feet.

Luckily the incident was seen by Mr Finch, from a window in the Pets' Home at the edge of the Palace grounds. Grasping a bottle of one of his own special mixtures, "Finch's Bird Reviver", he ran to the scene of the accident.

He was well experienced in looking after sickly
creatures, for he was the Keeper of the King's
Pets' Home, and was responsible for all the lost
and stray animals in the Great City.

'I have only used this Bird Reviver on small
City birds, sparrows, pigeons and starlings,' he
told the King, as he
poured the mixture
into Sally's beak.
'I hope it will

have effect on a big bird such as this.'

At that moment Sam appeared in the air above them.

'Lean well back!' cried Mrs Easter to Billie Guftie, as Sam nose dived. 'Lean well back! Or we shall surely slip over his head!'

The King was very surprised to see yet another stork descending, especially when he noticed that this one was carrying passengers.

The Sentry ran out of his sentry box to challenge them. 'Halt! Who goes there?' he demanded.

'Mrs Easter and Billie Guftie,' came the reply.

The Sentry did not seem satisfied with this answer and advanced upon them menacingly, pointing his rifle and frowning at them fiercely through his furry helmet. But when he saw the King step forward and graciously help Mrs Easter to dismount, he retired back into his sentry box.

Sam scampered eagerly towards Sally, who was still having Bird Reviver poured into her beak by Mr Finch.

Mrs Easter curtsied and Billie Guftie bowed.

'Welcome to my Palace!' said the King, cordially.

'It is unusual to travel on a stork's back. What made you choose this form of transport?'

Mrs Easter rose.

'We did not choose it, Your Majesty,' she replied, with a little smile. Then she and Billie Guftie told of their amazing journey.

When they had finished the King exclaimed, 'What courage! What a tale of romance! I am proud to receive such adventurers to my Palace!'

Just then a great commotion was heard and a large van came hurtling up the drive.

Billie Guftie recognized the driver at once. It was Burton! Burton in his Star Spotted Van!

'Who goes there?' challenged the Sentry, again advancing menacingly from his sentry box.

The King, who loved animals, often went to the Zoo, so he knew Burton well.

'Say "Pass friend!"' he ordered the Sentry. 'Pass friend!' said the Sentry rather reluctantly. He did not like vans driving up to the Palace. He would have preferred to have ordered Burton round to the back door.

Burton sprang from the van.

He gave a splendid salute which the King graciously acknowledged with a tweek of his crown.

'Your Majesty!' he said, rather breathlessly, for he had obviously been hurrying. 'I have just arrived from Denmark, where I have been hunting rare creatures for the Zoo. I was fortunate to capture one of the rarest of all birds, a stork with a luminous beak. I carried her in on the S.S.

114

Queenie, but, as we approached land, she struggled from my arms and flew into the sky. It has been reported to me that a strange light has been seen hovering over the Palace, so I hastened here.'

At that moment a triumphant shout was heard. They turned to see Mr Finch excitedly waving his bottle of Bird Reviver.

'It works! It works for big birds as well as little

birds!' he was shouting happily, as Sally rose radiantly from the ground.

When Burton saw her he gave a happy laugh. 'Hurrah! I've found her!' he cried, and ran towards her, as if to seize and capture her again.

But the King put a restraining hand on his shoulder.

'Burton,' he said, gravely, 'Do you know that Sally's husband, Sam, has just flown right across the mighty ocean to rescue her? Furthermore, throughout the journey, he carried on his back two passengers, Mrs Easter and her nephew, Billie Guftie.'

Burton recognized him. So once again Billie Guftie told the tale of the epic voyage.

'There,' said the King to Burton, 'Don't you agree with me that such devotion and courage on the part of this stork should be rewarded? And that his wife should go free?'

Burton was clearly moved by all he had heard, and, though he was disappointed that he would not have a stork with a luminous beak in the Zoo, he said, 'Gracious Monarch, you are wise and just. She shall go free!'

'Well spoken,' said the King, and everyone said, 'Hurrah!'

'They can sleep tonight in my Pets' Home!' said Mr Finch. 'For they will be too tired to fly again just yet.'

'I will take them there in my Star Spotted Van!' cried Burton. 'It is full of straw which will keep them warm.'

'Splendid!' said the King, and Billie Guftie led the birds to the van. To his astonishment, instead of getting into it, they each took a bundle of straw out of it in their beaks.

Then, to everyone's further astonishment, they soared into the air and landed on one of the ornamental chimneys of the Palace!

They left the straw on the chimney and flew down for more. Back they flew again. Down

again! Up again! Back again! Up again!

'What does this strange behaviour mean, Mr Finch?' asked the King, in bewildered tones.

'They are making a nest!' came the solemn reply. 'Your Majesty, it means they intend to live on your roof!'

'Then I am a most fortunate monarch!' said the King. 'I am sure there is no other King or Queen in the whole world who can boast of a stork's nest on one of their chimney-pots!'

He was so pleased that he grasped Billie Guftie and spun round in a merry dance.

Then he turned and said, 'Please enter my Palace one and all! We will celebrate this occasion with a tea-party!'

'What fun!' said Burton, as they hurried up the Palace steps, 'I am very fond of eating.'

'I am longing for a cup of tea,' said Mrs Easter.

They entered the drawing room through the french windows.

They all felt very happy when they saw the elegant table, laden with bread and butter, buns and chocolate biscuits.

The King took a saucer of milk and some éclairs which he placed on the balcony for the storks.

'They'll be hungry after all that nest-making,' he said. Then they sat down at the table and the King poured out the tea and handed round the buns and biscuits.

He offered Billie Guftie some delightful looking buns. 'They are called Matelot Hats, a speciality of the Palace,' he said. 'When I was a child I used to eat the bun part first, then the icing, and the cherry last of all. I don't do that any more now . . . now that I am grown up.'

'Oh! Please Your Majesty, let us do it today! As it is a special occasion,' cried Billie Guftie.

'What a good idea!' said the King.

So everyone took a Matelot Hat; and they all ate the bun part first, then the icing, and the cherry last of all.

Billie Guftie thought he had never enjoyed a tea

party so much. When it was time to go, Burton said to Mrs Easter: 'I will take you home in my van.'

'Thank you very much,' said Mrs Easter. 'Could you please stop at the Docks on the way, so that we can pick up our luggage from the S.S. *Queenie?*'

'Certainly,' replied Burton.

The King gave Billie Guftie a Matelot Hat to take home with him.

On the steps of the Palace they thanked the King for a wonderful tea-party.

'Today you have brought me great happiness,' he said, looking up at Sally and Sam who had just finished their nest.

'It is pleasant for a King to have a stork's nest on his Palace roof. But to have a stork with a luminous beak is really delightful. Think how pleased my people will be when they see this beautiful light brightening our City!'

Then after a certain amount of bowing and curtseying and murmuring of gracious words, Mrs Easter got into the Star Spotted Van and drove off with Burton.

As they passed the Sentry, he raised his rifle and held it in front of his face . . . a form of salute

reserved for important people and for people that the Sentry himself liked.

Further and further they drove from the Palace, but always Billie Guftie could see the light of Sally's beak shining over the Great City.

'How proud Mr and Mrs Jensen will be,' said Mrs Easter, 'when they hear that the storks that once nested on their little roof are now living on an ornamental chimney of a Royal Palace.'